To those, like us, who have trouble showing it.
—M. K. & R. L.

BLOOMSBURY CHILDREN'S BOOKS
Bloomsbury Publishing Inc., part of Bloomsbury Publishing Plc
1385 Broadway, New York, NY 10018

BLOOMSBURY, BLOOMSBURY CHILDREN'S BOOKS, and the Diana logo are trademarks of Bloomsbury Publishing Plc

First published in the United States of America in January 2022
by Bloomsbury Children's Books

Bloomsbury books may be purchased for business or promotional use. For information on bulk purchases
please contact Macmillan Corporate and Premium Sales Department at specialmarkets@macmillan.com

Library of Congress Cataloging-in-Publication Data
Names: Kerr, Mike, author. | Liwska, Renata, illustrator.
Title: Love is for roaring / by Mike Kerr ; illustrated by Renata Liwska.
Description: New York : Bloomsbury, 2022.
Summary: With help from his friend Mouse, Lion explores different
and sometimes unconventional ways to express his love.
Identifiers: LCCN 2021026263 (print) | LCCN 2021026264 (e-book)
ISBN 978-1-68119-124-9 (hardcover) • ISBN 978-1-68119-125-6 (e-book) • ISBN 978-1-68119-126-3 (e-PDF)
Subjects: CYAC: Lion—Fiction. | Mice—Fiction. | Love—Fiction. | LCGFT: Picture books.
Classification: LCC PZ7.1.K5097 Lo 2022 (print) | LCC PZ7.1.K5097 (e-book) | DDC [E]—dc23
LC record available at https://lccn.loc.gov/2021026263
LC e-book record available at https://lccn.loc.gov/2021026264

Illustrations drawn and colored digitally.
Typeset in Book Antiqua
Book design by Jeanette Levy
Printed in China by Leo Paper Products, Heshan, Guangdong
2 4 6 8 10 9 7 5 3 1

To find out more about our authors and books visit www.bloomsbury.com and sign up for our newsletters.

Love Is for

ROARING

MIKE KERR

ILLUSTRATED BY
RENATA LIWSKA

BLOOMSBURY
CHILDREN'S BOOKS
NEW YORK LONDON OXFORD NEW DELHI SYDNEY

The fearsome, fearless Lion faced the impossible,
the undoable, the unimaginable . . .

HOMEWORK:
Show your Love

"For whom? For what? And WHY?!" roared Lion.

"I don't like pink and I don't like hearts. I won't do it!"

The craft supplies made for one grumpy Lion.

Mouse sensed trouble. Lion snacked when he was stressed, and Mouse felt uncomfortably close.

"Um, Lion," Mouse squeaked, "what do you love? There must be something!"

"What's this about love?
Love is for doves and not for a lion!
I really don't love *love*!" said Lion.

"But . . . ," said Mouse, "how about . . ."

"Sweet treats, maybe?"
"Oh, no, I'm not fond of those!"

"Hmm, you don't say . . . ," replied Mouse to Lion.
But then he thought, *I wonder if there's another way?*

"How about running . . ."

".. . and playing?

You don't love that?"

"Or yawning, lounging, and dozing?" Mouse whispered. "You really don't love that?"

"Hey," said the teacher. "Who's snoring?"

"And growling, and roaring . . . You don't love that?

Okay, then chasing . . . and catching?"

"And are you sure you don't love . . .

. . . this?"

"On second thought . . . ," said Lion.

"*Hugs*? Not my favorite. *Kisses*? Not for me.

Treats? Not too sweet!"

"But maybe you're right, Mouse.

I love growling, and roaring, and
running, and chasing, and catching . . ."

Show your Love

"... and our friendship."

And the fearsome, fearless Lion wasn't afraid to show it.